Copyright © 2022 by Oronde A. Baylor

All rights reserved. This book or parts thereof may not be reproduced in any form, stored in any retrieval system, or transmitted in any form by any means—electronic, mechanical, photocopy, recording, or otherwise—without prior written permission of the publisher, except as provided by United States of America copyright law.

MALCOLM AKA CHUBBY HORNET
POWERS: GREEN TOXIC HONEY & POWER STING PUNCH
AGE:. 13

BRIT AKA THE WIZARD
POWERS: GENIUS, QUANTUM PHYSICS & TELEPORTATION
AGE: 8

SAM AKA THE FOX
POWERS: LIGHTNING FAST, SPEED, MARTIAL ARTS & PLUNGER LAUNCHER
AGE: 13

HONEYCOMB GIRLS: MI II, PEBBLES & PRETTY GIRL
POWERS: LULLABIES, BUBBLE BOMBS, SUPER SPEED & MARTIAL ARTS
AGES: 4

PROFESSOR BAYLOR
POWERS: GENIUS
AGE: UNKNOWN

HEFTY
POWERS: UNKNOWN
AGE: UNKNOWN

Professor Baylor, the science teacher at R. Grant Graham Middle School, watched his favorite news station.

Professor Baylor spits out his coffee when he hears on the news that everyone is missing a sock, and it's a sock monster on the loose!

Professor Baylor calls Malcolm and tells him that a sock monster is on the loose, eating everyone's socks!

Malcolm suddenly realizes his sock is missing!

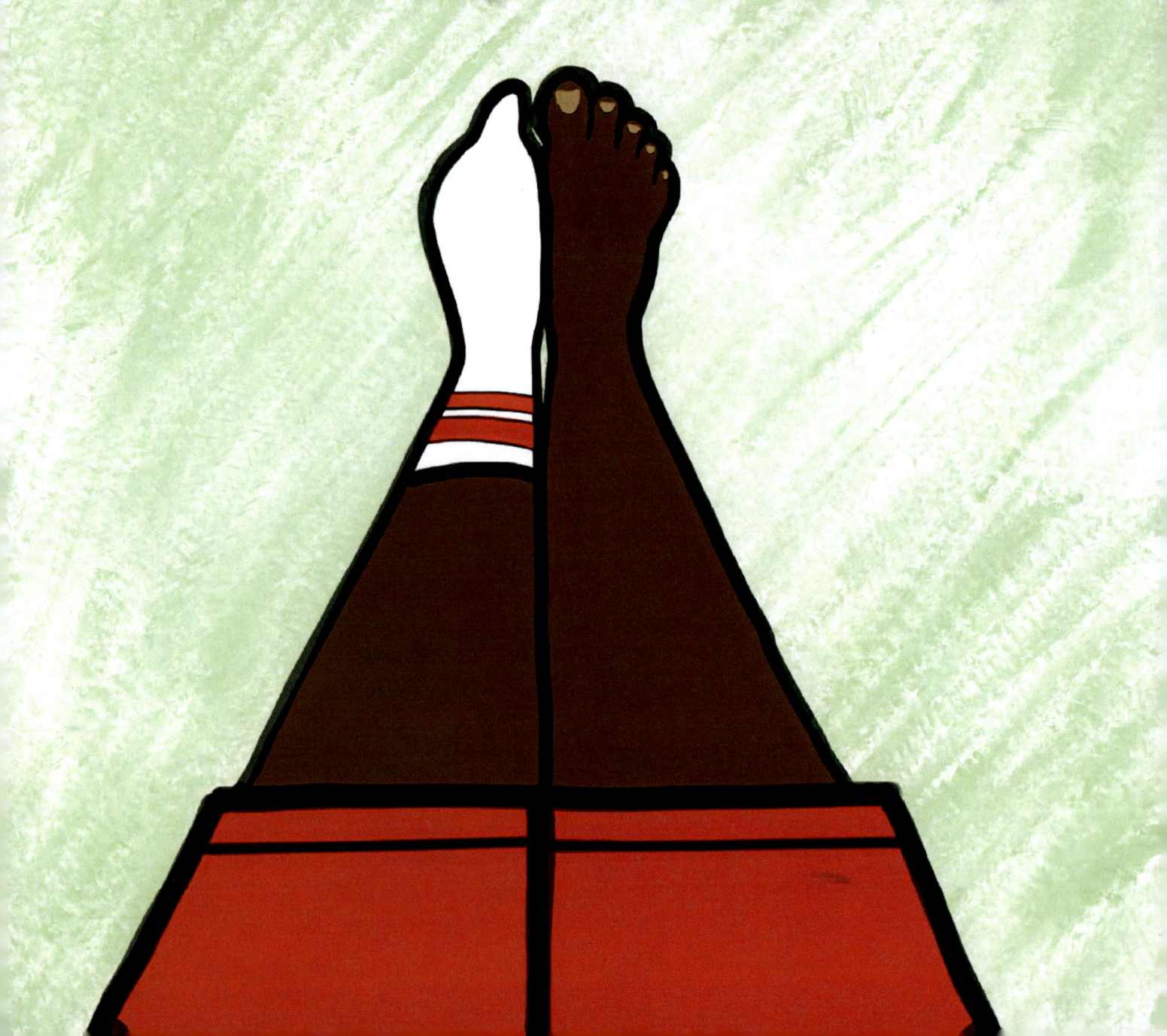

Malcolm sends a text message to Brit, Sam, and the Honeycomb Girls.

Group text:

Sock monster On the loose!

Report to Headquarters Immediately!!

He warns them of the sock monster and tells them to meet him at the Honeycomb Headquarters!

The sock monster has been spotted! He is eating everyone's socks, and no one can stop him!

3 DAYS EARLIER...

The Johnson family bought a new washing machine and threw the old one out in the alley behind their house. Walter, the washer, was sad because he was no longer needed.

A thunderstorm started in the middle of the night, and a lightning bolt struck Walter and turned him into the dreaded sock monster!

GRRRRR!!!!!

The sock monster is stealing socks from every home he passes. He continues to eat all the socks he can!

Malcolm and the Honeycomb Kids are planning how to catch the sock monster and force him into their trap!

Pretty Girl, Pebbles, and Mi II sing to the sock monster to calm him down!

Sam shoots her plunger and hits the sock monster in the mouth so he can't eat any more socks!

Sam, Brit, and Malcolm lead the sock monster into their trap!

🪙 Coin Laundry

Brit and Malcolm zap the sock monster with their green toxic honey and shrink him down to size.

Coin Laundry

The Honeycomb Kids put the old washer in the laundromat so he can retire peacefully with all of his friends. Walter the washer is very happy, thanks to the Honeycomb Kids!

Professor Baylor and the Honeycomb Kids remind you to recycle. If we don't recycle, we will have a monster on our hands!

MALCOLM

Honeycomb Quiz!!!

How many times did Hefty appear in the book?

Hefty

What is the sock monster's name?

How old is Sam?

Sam

Made in United States
North Haven, CT
19 June 2022